Murder
in the
Park

by

John Messingham

All rights reserved

The characters and events portrayed in this book are fictitious. Any similarity to real persons, living or dead, is coincidental and not intended by the author.

No part of this book may be reproduced, stored in a retrieval system, or transmitted in any form or by any means, electronic, mechanical, photocopying, recording, or otherwise, without the express written permission of the author.

Cover design by: John Messingham

This book is dedicated to Kiki.

Who used to sleep on the windowsill next to my writing desk while writing this.

One

There had been a heavy frost overnight and the sun had still to come up yet, so it was quiet in Grimsby's Peoples Park this morning. One elderly lady was out with her dog and had made her way around the park on her usual route past the lake and the bandstand and was now making her way back towards her home which was across the road from the park.

Her dog was still off its lead, running around and enjoying itself just as it did every morning during the walk it took with its owner. The dog owner was now making her way to the part of the path where she normally called her dog back to her so she could put its lead back on, so they could leave the park and cross the road safely and return home.

As she arrived at the point where she

usually turned to call her dog, she became aware of footsteps behind her.

Thinking it may be another dog walker she started to turn around, but, as she did the figure behind her rushed forwards and grabbed her.

She tried to scream out but as she did her attacker placed a hand over her mouth. She then felt herself being raised and pulled away from where she had been grabbed and into the trees to the side of the path.

The victim of the attack struggled but could not free herself from the grip of her attacker and once they were both away from the path, she felt something being placed around her neck.

She continued to struggle but found it harder and harder to do so as although she was not sure what had been put around her neck, she felt it getting tighter and tighter.

As the pressure on her neck grew, she felt weaker and weaker and eventually she could not fight back anymore. Once all the life had been drained from her body, the attacker lowered her to the ground and casually moved away. Walking at first and then breaking into a slow running pace as the attacker made their way around the park pathway and away into the morning darkness.

All the time the attack was taking place, the victim's dog could be heard barking and now just sat whimpering at the side of its owner, whose body was now just lying lifeless within the trees.

Two

DS Brierton and civilian staff member Allan Parsons were sitting in the team's office which was located within Grimsby's main police station. Things had been quiet for the last week or so which had enabled them to catch up with all their paperwork for the last couple of murder cases they had worked on.

The door of the office opened and in walked DCI Garner.

"Morning everyone," he said as he entered the office, closing the door behind him.

Both Brierton and Parsons looked up and Parsons said, "morning sir, good to see you back." To which Garner smiled and nodded in acknowledgement.

Brierton said, "how was your trip?"

Garner replied, "I can't go into much detail at this point but as you know I was in London."

Brierton said, "Yes, Superintendent Jones told us you had been sent down to work with the Metropolitan Police to assist them with an old case."

Garner said, "that's right, I'm sorry I could not say more at the time but because Mick Kurzwell had decided to become an informant it was all put on a need-to-know basis."

As Garner was speaking, he made his way to his desk and sat down. He then continued to speak.

"The National Crime Agency had arranged to allow a shipment of drugs to get through the port in Immingham but had followed it to the drop-off point in London. Then they arrested everyone involved and confiscated the drugs. I then went down and spent a day interviewing Kurzwell alongside the NCA so we could get enough evidence to put the remaining gang members away."

Parsons said, "so, does this go back to the big case you worked on when you were based in London?"

"Yes," Garner replied." I always knew a couple of the gang members had got away from us and I always felt disappointed that they had. But we got them in the end, even though it has taken a few years."

Brierton said, "and is this because of Kurzwell giving information about the remaining gang members?"

To which Garner replied, "yes, I remember saying to you before that I always thought he had a lot of information about them because he had started with the gang at quite a low position but moved up through the ranks."

Brierton then said, "so what made him change sides so to speak?"

Garner said, "He had become fearful for his life. The remaining members of the gang knew things were closing in on them, which is why they switched to using the port in Immingham to bring their drugs in and because Kurzwell knew so much about them and their operation, he thought he might be killed soon. It looked as if that is what was going to happen while he was in London as it was strange that he had been asked to go down with the drugs this time."

Parsons said, "I suppose that would have been a shame in a way because of the information he had, but on the other hand, it would not be a big loss."

Garner interrupted Parsons by saying, "I get your point but even with him out of the way, I doubt it will be long before another one takes over from him."

Brierton said, "true, I wonder how long it will be before we are all dealing with the fallout of that."

As Brierton had finished voicing her prediction for the future, Garner said, "right, let's get back to some kind of normality around here, seeing as it is quiet, let's go for a coffee."

Three

The team left their office and started to head for the station's canteen. As they did, Garner's mobile phone started ringing in his pocket. He took it out and while he was answering the call, he said, "Look at that, it's the control room. I've only been back two minutes and they are calling me already."

"DCI Garner," he announced and listened intently to the caller.

"Right, OK, we will head down there now," and ended the call.

He turned and looked towards Brierton and said, "We need to go down to the People's Park. A body has been found and they want us to go down and check the situation out."

Brierton said, "who was it who said it was all quiet around here?" and then looked at Parsons and said, "you had better go back to the office and prepare for some work."

Garner smiled at Brierton and said, "sorry, that'll teach me."

Both Garner and Brierton then headed down to the station car park to make their way down to the park where the body had been found and Parsons went back to the office.

As they left the station Garner said, "The control room said that other units and Rachael Howton have already been sent down so with a bit of luck we will know more of what has happened when we get there."

Four

Police tape had been stretched around a wooded area of the park where the dead body of a woman had been found. Rachel Howton had arrived at the scene a short while before and was preparing to examine the body and the surrounding area when Garner and Brierton arrived at the park.

As they approached Howton, she turned and said, "Crikey, you two are a bit quick off the mark, I have barely got my white suit on and you are already here."

Garner said, "maybe it's you that is getting a bit slower nowadays." To which Howton replied laughing, "I shan't even bother to tell you to suit up then, you just wait there and catch your breath."

After her verbal run-in with Garner,

Howton finished getting ready to approach the area where the body was lying, she pointed towards a woman standing near a police car that was parked across the road from the park talking to a uniformed officer and said, "While I get started I think you should speak to that lady over there. I think she was the one who found the body and called us."

Brierton replied, "OK, I'll go and speak to her."

As Brierton walked away from Garner and Howton, Howton asked Garner, "how was your trip to London? Is that all moving forward now?"

To which Garner replied, "yes, it all went well. The case is being prepared for the court which will hopefully start within the next few months."

Howton said, "that's good. Right then, I'll get started here and get back to you as soon as I have something. I guess you will want everything just before as soon as possible as usual." She then chuckled under her breath and walked towards the area of the woods where the body was located. Pulling her trolley of plastic boxes behind her as she walked.

Once Garner had been left alone, he looked around where he stood and could see that everything that needed to be done to secure the scene had indeed been done, so he made his way to where Brierton was talking to the woman who had found the body.

Five

Garner had made his way over to where Brierton and a uniformed officer were talking to a female dog walker who had found the body. Brierton had been talking to her and had now asked the officer with them to carry on and take a full statement and send it to her as soon as possible.

Brierton said, "this is Helen, she walks her dog here most mornings and it was her dog that had drawn her attention to the body."

Garner looked over towards Helen and said, "morning, this must all be a real shock for you, are you OK?"

Helen looked towards Garner and nodded her head which Garner took as her saying yes. He then looked towards the uniformed officer and said, "can we maybe arrange some tea for Helen, while you take her statement, please?" and then turned back towards Brierton, and under his breath he said.

"and us, it's flipping freezing. Right, what have you got?"

Brierton said, "not much really, she was walking her dog when it went into the trees over there and started barking for some reason. When she went into the trees to find her dog and to see what was going on she found the body and called us immediately."

Garner said, "does she know who it is?"

Brierton replied, "no, she has seen the dog about and the lady that walks it most mornings but has never got to know her or even said much more than hello to her. She was able to get the victim's dog away from the body as she thought it may help to calm it down a bit as it seemed upset, as to be expected."

Garner said, "right, OK then. Let's see if we can get a warm cuppa and then go back and speak to Howton and see what she has for us."

Brierton agreed by saying, "OK, probably best not to rush her."

Six

A small crowd had now gathered along the road that went around the park near where the police had put up more police tape. Uniformed officers had taken up positions along the tape to stop people from being able to interfere with the work being carried out within the cordon.

As Garner and Brierton headed back across the road after speaking to the person who found the body one of the officers said, "there are lots of people asking what is going on, is there anything we can tell them, sir?"

Garner said in response, "I'm afraid not, we have to make initial enquiries and let any family members know what has happened before we start making public statements."

The officer nodded at this and replied, "OK, Sir, we will carry on telling them that an incident has taken place in the park but no details are being released at the moment."

After this short exchange, Garner and Brierton carried on making their way over to where Howton was still working on gathering evidence from the murder scene.

Howton was still hunched over the body found in the park when Garner and Brierton arrived back at the taped scene.

Garner called over to her, "have you got anything?"

Howton looked up and said jokingly, "have you had one of those energy drinks this morning? You can't just wait can you." To which Garner replied, "I just know how much you like to be hurried, especially at this time of the day."

Howton walked over to where Garner and Brierton were standing carrying an evidence bag in her hand and once she was standing near the police tape, she said, "bet you wouldn't be so cheeky if this tape was not here to protect you. Anyway, here is a bunch of keys the victim had in her pocket." As she spoke she passed the bag to Brierton saying, "you had better have this Becca, he is in such a hurry he will probably lose it, and the keys."

Garner just laughed and Brierton said, "thanks, " and started to look at the contents of the bag.

Garner then said, "victim? You're sure we have a victim and not just a sudden or unexplained death?"

Howton replied to this with, "definitely a victim, she has a lot of fresh bruising around the neck so I am sure we are dealing with murder here. I don't think it happened very long ago either as the body is still very warm to the touch, So I would hazard a guess in that the attack took place within the last couple of hours."

Garner took a moment to take this in and then said to Howton, "right, I don't suppose there was anything on the victim that would identify them?" Howton just shook her head at this, so Garner looked towards Brierton and continued, "can you get the house-to-house started straight away so we can find out if anyone knows who the victim might be."

Brierton nodded and said, "will do," and walked away from Garner and Howton towards the area of the park where most of the assembled officers were now waiting.

Seven

Brierton had organised a small group of officers who had been sent down to the park to see if they could assist with the investigation to start visiting the houses surrounding the park and see if anyone had seen, heard or could identify the victim.

Brierton had decided to get all the officers to take a photo of the victim's dog which was now being kept in the back of a police car nearby on their smartphones so this could be shown to residents rather than an image of the body.

As the house-to-house enquiries progressed Brierton arrived at a house almost directly opposite where the body had been found. She knocked on the door and waited for an answer.

After a short time, the door of the house opened and a middle-aged woman wearing a loosely tied, thin dressing gown that showed that she was only wearing a small nightie underneath.

As the resident realised it was the police standing on her doorstep she quickly pulled the front of the dressing gown closed and tied it tighter and said, "Hello, sorry, can I help you?"

Brierton gave the lady time to sort her apparel out and then said.

"Morning, we are carrying out house-to-house enquiries as unfortunately the body of an older lady was discovered in the park this morning. Can you recall hearing or seeing anything unusual in the early hours of the morning?"

The lady pondered for a moment and said, "No, but both myself and my mother sleep in rooms at the back of the house."

As she was speaking a young man walked up the garden path and stood behind Brierton.

"What's going on Sasha?" the young man

asked.

Brierton turned towards the young man and said, "We have found a body in the park, have you been around here long this morning?"

The young man replied, "no, I have just arrived and was coming here to carry on with the decorating in Sasha's mum's house."

Sasha then said, "you had better come in Peter if you have nothing to tell the police. Sam is already here and working."

As Sasha said this, Peter made his way past Brierton and into the hallway of the house. Brierton noticed that as he entered the house, Sasha moved slightly into his path and smiled at him saying, "you look hot, have you been running this morning?" Peter had to squeeze past Sasha and as he did so, she pulled his woolly hat off and threw it at him.

Eight

While Brierton was getting on with the house-to-house and Howton carried on examining the victim's body and the area around it, Garner had received a call and was told to head back to the station as his boss, Superintendent Jones, wanted to speak to him in person.

Garner was soon back in the station and sitting outside the Superintendent's office, waiting to be called in.

After a few minutes, the door of the Superintendent's office opened and Superintendent Jones asked Garner to come in.

As he entered the office, Garner noticed that another person was also sitting in the office with their back towards the door. Garner could not miss the fact that this person had the phrase 'NCA' on the back of their jacket so straight away assumed this meeting was about his recent trip to London linked to the historical case he had been helping the National Crime Agency with.

"This is Elena Bendel from the National Crime Agency," said Superintendent Jones as she made her way back around her desk and sat down.

Garner said, "hello Elena," as he sat down at the desk next to Elena.

"Elena is in charge of the NCA team dealing with Mick Kurzwell while they wait for the court to set a date for the case to be heard, " said Jones and then looked towards Elena and continued, "I'll let you carry on with this briefing."

Elena said, "thank you, ma'am," and turning to Garner said, "we are hoping to get this case in front of a judge as soon as possible but have hit a problem. You see, it's possible that the location of the safe house where Kurzwell was staying was compromised and we needed to move him quickly."

Garner replied to this with, "I guess the fact you are here means he is around here somewhere."

To which Elena replied, "yes, we have moved him back up here because everybody who was involved with him thinks he is still in London now. So we are hoping the people looking for him will just think we have moved him to another London safe house."

Garner then asked, "do you know how the safe house might have been compromised? Do you think someone in your organisation is leaking information?"

Elena said, "we are still trying to work out what happened. All we know is that the team looking after him, spotted a known associate of the other people in custody in the area of the safe house. So, to be safe, we have moved Kurzwell."

Superintendent Jones said, "that's pretty much it Robert. I know you are dealing with the People's Park case at the moment but we wanted you to know what was going on."

Garner said, "OK, Will you keep me

updated on the Kurzwell situation?"

Elena said, "we will, and thank you for all your help on this. It was a great help when you came down to London to interview him as your knowledge of the original case proved invaluable.

Garner stood up from his chair and said, "thanks, I expect I'll see you again soon, " and left the Superintendent's office to make his way back to the team's office to see what was happening on the current case.

Nine

Back at the house where Brierton was talking to Sasha, she was just about to show Sasha the image of the dog when another female voice called from a room on the first floor of the house.

"What's going on down there? Who are you talking to?"

Sasha said, "that's my mother, she is very ill at the moment."

Brierton said, "I'm sorry to hear that, would it be possible for me to speak to her? In case she heard something this morning."

Sasha replied, "would you mind not doing that? Anyway, her bedroom is at the back of the house so I doubt she would have heard anything. She is also taking sleeping pills to help her sleep, so I would not expect she has anything to tell you."

Brierton said, "OK, maybe you could ask her yourself and give me a call if she has any information that may help us."

Sasha said she would do that and asked, "is there anything else?"

Brierton then raised her phone and using it showed Sasha the image of the dog she had opened on the device.

Sasha said, "That's Cindy. Goodness, that's Miriam's Cindy. Is that who you've found in the park?"

Brierton said, "we have not made a formal identification yet but knowing who the dog belongs to will most likely help us do that now. Do you know where Miriam lives?"

Sasha had started to cry now and struggled to speak but said, "yes, she lives at number 38. I cannot believe it may be her, she and my mum have been friends for years."

Brierton said, "right, OK. If I need to speak to you again, I will be in touch and please speak to your mother to see if she heard anything this morning and if she did please call me," and handed Sasha a business card that had her contact details printed on.

Ten

Brierton had called Garner to tell him they had a possible identification for the victim and he had now made his way back down to the park and arrived outside Miriam's house. They had no idea if she lived alone or if there would be other people in the house. If there was, then they were going to have to deliver the bad news themselves.

Once at the front door of the house, Brierton rang the doorbell. They waited a short while and then rang the bell for a second time to which once again came no reply. So, to give anyone in the house one more chance to open the door Brierton knocked on it and rang the bell one more time. Once again there was no answer so she placed a rubber glove on her hand and took a set of keys out of the evidence bag Howton had handed to her. She then used one of the keys to open the door and both she and Garner walked into the house.

After a few minutes of walking around Miriam's house, Garner and Brierton were satisfied there was no one in the property and apart from an empty wine bottle and two wine glasses on the living room coffee table, the house was very tidy they did not think anything untoward had taken place within the house so they headed back out of the property, locking the front door behind them.

As they walked away from the house, Garner said, "you had better take those keys back to Rachel Howton, she will want to have a longer look around the house to be sure nothing happened that we could not see."

Brierton replied, "OK, sir. I'll go and see her as soon as we get back. I will ask her to come out as soon as she can. I will not tell her we went all around the house though as you know what she gets like if she is not first in."

Garner said, "good point, I don't fancy a spell in her bad books. I'll head back to the office and see if any relatives have been located so that we can contact them and break the bad news to them. They may even be able to give us an insight into the victim's life which may help us find out why she has been murdered."

They both then made their way back to the car and headed back to the station.

Eleven

A couple of miles away in another popular dog walking area. A dog walker was being confronted by a man who had seemingly been running around the park and been tripped up by a dog running across his path.

An officer and community support officer had been sent down to deal with the situation and had made their way to the area. One of them was talking to the owner of the dog and the other was taking a statement from the runner.

The dog owner said, "I don't think the dog was anywhere near him, to be honest. So I cannot imagine why he is making such a fuss. I think he just fell over and is looking to blame someone to save face."

The community support officer then said,

"so, did you see the runner fall over?"

To which the owner replied, "that's the thing, no, and as I said before, I don't think the dog ever went near him. All I know is he came running up to me shouting that bloody dog owners should be strung up using their dog's leads, as they are a nuisance in public spaces."

The community support officer continued, "OK if you can just wait here sir, I will go and speak to my colleague and then see where we go from here," and then made their way over to where the other officer was talking to the runner. The officer turned and said, "this gentleman claims the dog whose owner you were talking to tripped him up. What is he saying?"

The community support officer said, "well, the dog owner claims he did not see the dog trip the runner up."

As the community support officer spoke, the runner said, "well, I guess you're not going to do anything about this so I may as well go home." To which the officer said, "can you wait here for a moment sir."

As the officer finished speaking, the runner turned and started to move away from them and so the officers had to move quickly to stop him. A struggle ensued but the officers were able to get the runner to the floor and held him there while the officer called back to the station to request assistance.

Within a few minutes, a police van arrived at the scene with another couple of officers who took hold of the runner who had now been placed under arrest and led him to the rear of the van.

Once the runner had been placed into the back of the police van, the community support officer went over to the dog owner and said.

"We will need you to attend an interview at the police station. This is because there was a threat of violence towards you and we need a formal interview to be recorded. Are you heading home now?"

The dog owner replied, "yes." To which the community support officer replied, "that's fine. I will arrange for a car to come and pick you up shortly and take you to the station."

Twelve

Rachel Howton had now arrived at the team's office and made her way across the room to a chair near Garner's desk.

The rest of the team was standing near Garner's desk talking about the case and once Howton had sat down she started to speak.

"The bruising I showed you at the scene was created while the killer strangled the victim. The murder weapon was some kind of thin woven strap, no more than an inch wide."

Brierton said, "we searched the area around the body and the rest of the park is being searched now, but nothing like that was found. So maybe the killer took it with them after the attack."

Howton then continued, "right, if you find anything fitting the description, it should be possible to confirm if it is the murder weapon as we have fibre samples from the victim's neck. I also found some dark fibres on the victim's hands that appear to be wool as well. I will get back to you when I have had a longer look at them."

Garner was just about to say something when Brierton's mobile telephone started to ring.

Brierton took her phone out of her pocket and as she answered the call and placed the phone to her ear she walked away from where the team were gathered. As she did, she said.

"Hello, DS Brierton. Can I help you?"

As Brierton took her call, Garner said.

"Was there any evidence of anything else taking place at the murder scene?"

To which Howton answered, "no, there is no evidence of anything other than strangulation having taken place."

Brierton had now come back to the team

after ending her call and said, "that was a lady called Sasha Bryon who lives with her mum Geraldine Bryon across the road from the park. I spoke to her during the house-to-house enquiries. She called to say she had spoken to her mum but she had not heard anything in the early hours of the morning. She did mention something that she thinks might be of interest to us about another neighbour, Anita Pemble, who had visited her mum the night before and was very upset. She said, Anita Pemble had been having an affair with the victim and been given an ultimatum about leaving her husband and moving away with her."

Parsons said, "well that would certainly give her the motive to kill Miriam."

To which Garner replied, "true, and when we visited the victim's house, there was the wine bottle and glasses in the living room. Which may confirm that Anita had visited the victim the night before."

Howton looked towards Garner and with a glaring stare said, "I guess I will need to ignore either of your two's fingerprints on them or anywhere else in the house then."

As Howton headed out of the office another officer walked in past her and said, "sir, we are holding a male suspect downstairs. He was brought in after an altercation with a dog walker. He was arrested because he made physical threats towards the dog owner that suggested he may have been involved in the People's Park incident.

Brierton said, "what were the threats made?"

To which the officer replied, "he said dog walkers should all be strung up using their dog's leads. We are checking out his alibi for the time of the murder but thought you would want to know."

Garner said, "yes, thanks for that. Can you let us know if his alibi does not work out?"

The officer replied, "yes, sir. I will update you as soon as I can," and then left the office, closing the door behind him.

Garner then turned to Brierton and said, "can you arrange for Anita to be brought in, it looks like she may be the last person to see the victim before she was killed."

Thirteen

Anita Pemble and her solicitor had been sitting in the interview room for about ten minutes when Garner and Brierton walked in and sat down at the table opposite them.

Brierton switched on the recording device on the table and said, "interview with Anita Pemble, her legal representative, DCI Garner and myself, DS Brierton."

Garner then said, "hello Anita," to which she just nodded, Garner continued, "we would like to talk to you about your relationship with Miriam Parris. Now I'm sure you have been told to make no comments to our questions, but I don't think this will help you in this case."

Brierton then asked, "can you tell us the nature of your relationship with Miriam?"

Anita replied, "I know I am supposed to say 'No Comment' but we were just friends. We walked our dogs together from time to time and had the odd cup of coffee but that was it."

Garner then said in a slightly softer than usual tone, "I appreciate this may be a delicate question, seeing that you are a married woman but, we have received information that suggests your relationship with Miriam was more of a romantic nature than what you just described to us. Do you have anything to say about that?"

Anita now had a shocked look on her face and said, "I do not know who would tell you that because that is simply not the case. We have known each other a long time and like I said we walked our dogs together from time to time but I can assure you that is all. There has never been anything romantic between us."

Anita now started to raise her voice a bit and continued, "I have been married to Edward for a long time and we are still very much in love and very happy."

Garner then said, "right OK, we will need to look into this further then to see if we have been misled or not. For now, though, can you confirm where you were at around sunrise this morning?"

Anita replied, "well, I was tucked up in bed with my husband if you really must know?"

"OK, thank you for that. I take it your husband will confirm that?" Garner replied and looking at Brierton, said, "we'll leave this for now but will need you to wait here while we check what you have said."

Brierton turned towards the recording system and said, "interview terminated," and pressed the stop button on the device.

Garner and Brierton then left the interview room and stopped in the corridor outside.

Brierton said, "do you want me to get her husband brought in for questioning? If there was more to Anita and Miriam's relationship, it is always possible that her husband found out about it and the ultimatum Miriam had given Anita and decided to stop the relationship from becoming public."

Garner thought for a while and then said, "yes, bring him in. We need to confirm her alibi anyway. Although, if they are both involved, it is going to be extremely hard to prove if they are going to give each other an alibi."

Once Garner had finished speaking, Brierton headed down the corridor towards the exit to the car park and Garner started to make his way back to the team's office.

Fourteen

Brierton had driven back to the area of the People's Park and had arrived at Anita and Edward's house where officers were in the process of searching the house. Brierton walked into the house and made her way to the front living room where Edward was sitting while the search was taking place.

Brierton beckoned two of the officers in the house to follow her into the room.

As Brierton entered the room, Edward stood up and said, "when will they be finished? I want to go down to the police station to see if my wife is OK."

Brierton said, "they will be finished when they have finished searching the whole house.

On the subject of going down to the police

station, we would like to speak to you down there anyway about the case, so we can clear up some statements made by your wife. So, if you could go with these officers they will drive you down now and I will join you as soon as I get back to the station myself."

"Why do you want to speak to me?"

"As I said, we want to clear up some things your wife has said. So, if you could go with these two officers, I will get back to the station as soon as I can."

"I suppose if it will get this all over and done with quicker I will go with you."

Edward then left the room following one officer and the other then followed on behind him as they left the house and went towards a police car parked outside.

Brierton stopped and stood in the hallway of the house while the other officers searched.

Now and then an officer would pass Brierton but so far nothing had been found that looked related to the investigation.

Suddenly, a voice from an upstairs room called out.

"Sarge, up here."

Brierton turned towards the staircase leading to the upstairs of the house and made her way up to where the voice had called from.

"Were are you?" She called out.

"In the front bedroom," the voice continued.

Brierton entered the front bedroom of the house where two uniformed officers were standing near a bedside table.

One of the officers pointed towards the bedside table and said, "We thought this might be something you would want to see."

As the officer spoke, Brierton looked towards the table and saw a thin brown woven dog lead coiled up within the top drawer that the officer had opened partly to reveal its contents.

"Right," Brierton said, "let's get that into

an evidence bag. It certainly fits the description of what we believe to be the murder weapon but we need to be sure. Whose bedside table is that?"

As Brierton spoke, the officer pulled a plastic evidence bag out of his pocket and with his already rubber-gloved hand, placed the lead into the evidence bag and sealed the bag up and said, "it looks like the husband's side."

Brierton said, "Thanks, I'll take this straight back to the station with me now and pass it on to the forensics team."

Fifteen

Garner and Anita's husband Edward Pemble were both sitting in an interview room waiting for Brierton who had come back to the station after dropping off the lead to join them.

She entered the room and sat down beside Garner who was sitting opposite Edward.

Brierton said, "sorry to keep you both waiting," then started the recording system in the room and then asked Edward, "are you sure you do not want legal representation during this interview?"

Edward responded, "no, it's fine. I have not done anything wrong so I am not worried."

Brierton carried on by saying, "OK, as you know you are here voluntarily and not under arrest so you can leave at any time you wish. Do you understand that?"

Edward responded with a simple nod and said, "yes, I understand."

"Can you confirm where you were at about six am this morning?"

"Yes, I was tucked up in bed with my wife at that time."

Brierton said, "I guess there is no one that can confirm that?"

To which Edward sarcastically replied, "we don't have that sort of lifestyle I am afraid, do you?"

Brierton thought about the last comment made by Edward but decided the situation was too serious for her to reply 'No comment' for a change. So she just went with, "can you explain why a dog lead matching the description of the murder weapon was found in your bedroom?"

Edward thought for a moment and then said, "not really, I don't know what the description of the murder weapon is. Anyway, our dog died a few months ago so I am not sure how you found a dog lead in the bedroom as we had gathered up all the things linked to the dog back then and asked someone to take them away because Anita found having them around the house upsetting."

As Garner and Brierton carried out the interview, the interview room door opened and Parsons stuck his head around the door and said.

"Can I speak to you both please?"

Garner said, "OK, interview suspended while DCI Garner and DS Brierton step out of the room."

Brierton stopped the recording and both she and Garner got up from the table and went outside the room, leaving the door open so they could see back into it.

Sixteen

Garner and Brierton joined Parsons outside the interview room in the corridor.

Parsons said, "sorry to bother you both during an interview but I have been through a lot of the doorbell and CCTV camera footage from around the park. It has taken some time because almost every house around the park has one fitted, in some cases more than one."

Brierton said, "what have you got for us?"

Parsons continued, "I was working through them and came across what appears to be a male jogger running away from the murder scene area at about the time we think the attack took place. So, I checked other camera footage and some of the CCTV from other houses and it does look like the jogger may have been in the right place at the right time to have at least heard something."

Garner said, "have you got the footage ready to be sent out to everyone still out near the park so they show it to people?"

To which Parsons responded with, "yes, I have also printed some screenshots showing the jogger from a couple of different angles. They don't show a lot of detail but there may be enough to jog somebody's memory of who it is if you'll pardon the pun." And handed Brierton the paper prints of the images from the video.

Garner said, "great, get them sent out to the officers on the ground as well to see if anyone knows the person."

Parsons agreed and went off back to the team's office to send the video and images out to officers that were still in the area.

Garner looked at Brierton who was studying the images closely and said, "you look as if you have recognised something."

Brierton replied, "yes, I am sure I have

seen this outfit somewhere before but cannot think of where. It may just be a common running outfit but it looks so familiar as if I have seen someone wearing it recently."

Just as they were going to return to the interview room to continue talking to Edward, Garner's mobile pinged, signalling he had a new text message. Once he had looked at the message he said, "we need to also go back to the office as Rachael is coming over to update us on what she found from the house."

Brierton replied, "OK, I will tell Edward and his solicitor they will have to wait a bit and then catch you up."

Seventeen

After Brierton had spoken to Edward and his solicitor she started to make her way back to the office. As she passed through the reception area of the station one of the reception staff called out.

"DS Brierton, the lady over there is here to speak to you."

As Brierton looked towards the reception, the staff member that had called out pointed towards a lady sitting in a chair opposite the reception desk. Brierton made her way over and spoke to the lady.

"I'm DS Brierton, can I help you."

As Brierton spoke to the lady she stood up and said, "Hello, I'm Freda Anderson. I would like to speak to you about my sister. Miriam Parris."

Brierton took a moment to take in who was standing in front of her, enquiries had been made but no one had been aware that Miriam had a sister. She knew that in the next few moments, things could be a bit embarrassing.

"Hello, I am sorry to meet you under the present circumstances, " Brierton said, and then decided to bring up the point they were unaware of her existence straight away by saying, "we had made enquiries but had not been able to find any relatives of Miriam."

To Brierton's surprise, Freda took this statement with no real surprise.

Freda said, "That's not a surprise, I was born a few years before Miriam and put up for adoption because of our mum's age at the time. We only got in touch with each other about six months ago when a friend of Miriam's was going through an old diary of their mothers and found an entry that mentioned me, my mum, and the adoption. Miriam then spent the last couple of years trying to find me. I was going round to see her this morning and one of the neighbours told me what had happened so I came straight here."

Brierton said, "I see, let me see if we can get a room so we can speak further in private and I will see if my boss wants to join us."

To which Freda responded with, "OK, that would be great. This has all been a bit of a shock to me. We only got to meet a couple of times over the last few months and then this happens."

Brierton turned back towards the reception and asked, "is there a free interview room?" The member of staff sitting behind the reception desk pointed towards a room attached to the reception area of the station.

Brierton looked towards the room and indicated to Freda to go towards it and through the door. Once Freda had sat down in the room, Brierton said, "I will just go and speak to my boss as I am sure he will want to join us, can I get you a drink, tea, coffee or water?"

"I'm fine, thank you."

Brierton then left Freda in the office alone while she went to call Garner to tell him about Freda turning up at the station.

Eighteen

The reception area of the police station had suddenly become very busy. There were uniformed officers running past and heading out of the station.

Brierton stood by the reception desk and asked the staff working there, "What's going on?"

"We have another rooftop protest taking place?" One of the staff answered, "I think most of the staff in this place are trying to get down there in case they miss out on the free pizzas."

"I hope none of the guys down at the People's Park catch wind of this or they will be heading there as well."

Once this exchange had finished Brierton asked, "can I use one of your phones, please?"

This request was met with another member of the reception staff passing Brierton one of the telephones sitting on the desk and saying, "sure, there you go."

Brierton picked up the handset and dialled the internal number for her team's office.

"Hi, " she said, "is the boss there?" she asked and waited for a reply.

"Hello sir, I am down at the reception. It turns out that Miriam Parris has a sister and she's here at the station."

Brierton stopped speaking to give Garner a chance to take this news in and then asked, "do you want to come down and speak to her with me?"

Garner had said he wanted her to wait in reception for him so he could come down and they could speak to Freda together.

Brierton said, "OK, I'll wait here so we can speak to her together." She then replaced the phone handset on the base unit and pushed it back towards the reception staff, saying, "thanks," as she did so.

Nineteen

The door to the interview room where Miriam's sister Freda was sitting opened and in walked Garner and Brierton.

"This is DCI Garner," Brierton announced as they walked in and Garner closed the door behind him.

"Hello, I am very sorry about what has happened to your sister and that you had to find out about it in the way you did."

Freda replied, "it's OK, it could not be helped. I do not live in the area so had not heard the news. I had arranged to visit Miriam last week and drove up this morning."

Garner continued, "well, we have a couple of people helping us with our enquires but unfortunately are still not sure why she was killed as yet."

Freda said, "I don't think there will be anything I can say that will help you. From the conversations I had with her over the last few months, I got the impression she kept herself to herself most of the time. Well, since the death of her husband last year. She mentioned some of the neighbours had been kind to her since his death but to be honest she didn't seem to like many of them that much."

Brierton said, "I know this is prying a bit but we trying to understand as much as we can about Miriam. We have information that suggests she was in a relationship with Anita Pemble. Did she ever mention anything about this to you?"

Freda thought for a moment and then said, "Unless she was embarrassed to say something, I would be very surprised if that was the case. I know you cannot always be sure what goes on behind closed doors but from what I know about my sister, she is more likely to have an affair with Edward Pemble, but to be honest, I doubt even that would be a possibility as she didn't like them very much. She called them the Pemble Pains as they always wanted to know everything she was doing."

Garner said, "That's very helpful," and got up from the chair he was sitting in," I will leave you with DS Brierton who can run you through how we can help you in this situation. Are you staying in the area for now? or will you be heading home?"

Freda looked up at Garner and said, "I will stay here for now as I suppose I will need to arrange the funeral and speak to Miriam's solicitor if there is one. Do you know what I will have to do to confirm who I am, I appreciate you have taken what I have said in good faith but I assume I will have to formally prove who I am in some way."

As Garner started to leave the room he said, "that's fine, DS Brierton can help you with all of that as we have the details of Miriam's solicitor and we can arrange for someone to take you down to the town hall so you can speak to them about being recorded as the next of kin."

Once Garner had left the room, Brierton explained to Freda what would happen next from the police's point of view and then asked her to wait in the room and she would ask someone from reception to arrange a car that could take her down to the town hall.

Brierton thanked Freda for her help and said she would keep in touch with her so she could be kept up to date with any developments in the case.

Twenty

As Garner passed through the reception area of the police station. He noticed Elena Bendel standing near the exit talking to Superintendent Jones. When Jones saw Garner she beckoned him over to where she was standing with Elena. Garner made his way over and joined them.

Elena said, "we are just about to take Kurzwell back to London as we have managed to get a court hearing arranged for tomorrow so we can put all the evidence we have gathered before a judge."

Garner said, "that's great, so, all being well and good, all the suspects you have in custody can be remanded until a full hearing can be arranged."

Elena replied, "yes, I just wanted to pop in and ask Superintendent Jones to pass on our thanks once again to you for all your help. But seeing as we have bumped into each other, I can thank you in person."

Jones said, "So, do you think Robert will need to go down to London at some point?"

To which Elena replied, "I doubt it. We would not have got as much evidence as we have without DCI Garner's help. But with some of them opening up with information about each other to try and save themselves from longer sentences, I expect we will get all the convictions we want."

Jones replied, "that's good. Well, I will let you get on with your travels and look forward to hearing from you in the future."

Garner said, "I must get on as well. I have got to have a team briefing about the People's Park murder case. We have a lot of information coming in but still cannot get a solid lead. So I will say goodbye."

Once Garner had finished talking he shook Elena's hand and started to walk away behind Jones who was now leaving the reception area. Elena headed out of the station exit to make her way back to London. As Garner crossed the reception area Brierton caught up with him and said.

"That's Freda Anderson on her way to the town hall. Are you heading back to the office?"

Garner replied, "eventually, I feel the need to have a drink and get my thoughts together on the case. Are you joining me?"

Brierton said, "will do, I'll call Allan and get him to join us." As she spoke they passed the reception desk and Brierton asked the staff member on the desk, "how's the protest going?"

The member of staff at the reception desk shrugged their shoulders and said, "it's ongoing."

Garner said, "what's that?"

To which Brierton responded, "there's a

rooftop protest taking place on the Cleethorpes road."

Garner said, "oh well, at least the canteen will be quiet, for a change."

Twenty-One

The building opposite the Albion public house which for many years sat derelict but now was covered in scaffolding while being renovated had become the scene of the latest rooftop protest in Grimsby.

Cleethorpes Road had been shut both ways to give uniformed officers and a negotiator a safe area to work. A protester had used the scaffolding around the building to gain access to the rooftop area of the building and was refusing to come down.

Officers in full riot suits and carrying Shields so they could protect themselves from the slates the protester was hurling down at them were standing around near the bottom of the building ready to enter and make their way up to the roof area if ordered to do so.

Off to the side of the building stood a police sergeant and an officer that was a trained negotiator and had been tasked with talking to the protester to try and talk him into coming down peacefully. This did not seem to be the first thing on the protester's mind as he hurled another slate down towards the officers who all moved so that the slate narrowly missed them.

"Come on mate, let's call it a day so we can all go and get a cuppa." Shouted the negotiator.

The protester lent over the scaffolding so he could get a good aim at the officers below and shouted, "NO, I ain't coming down until all my demands are met."

"Well, what are your demands?" shouted back the negotiator.

"I haven't decided yet, so you'll have to wait." Came back from the rooftop.

The negotiator turned towards the sergeant who was standing with him and said, "this is going to be a long one isn't it?"

To which the Sergeant replied, "yep, I guess so. He is probably upset because the Albion is probably going to be a shop and not a pub. Anyway, I'll go and call the station and see if I can get a command van sent down and a food truck if possible."

As the Sergeant made his way away from being on the target area of the protester, more tiles came crashing down, missing him by only a few feet. He then called the station using his mobile telephone to ask for the extra vehicles to be sent down.

While he was making this call, he asked if someone could find out how many tiles were in the roof area. He asked this as someone had noticed that the roof of the building was still open but it was possible to see piles of tiles in the roof area of the building.

"OK, if you can let me know. I will get someone to try and keep a count of the tiles coming down so we get an idea of when he is running out. You had better let the builders know they will need to order some more."

The Sergeant ended his call and headed

back to where the negotiator was now standing, he had moved further away from the building as the protester appeared to have improved his aim.

"They are going to arrange the command vehicle but I don't think there will be a food truck coming down so we may have to get a couple of other officers to start making trips to the local cafes." The Sergeant said.

"Ouch, " one of the officers standing near the building cried out. He had been struck on the helmet by one of the tiles.

"He's OK, " came another voice in the same area.

The Sergeant heard this and called over to the group of officers, "pull back for now. We will carry on trying to talk him down, but if he stops throwing tiles, can you sort out a couple of targets for him to aim at from time to time? If talking does not work, at least then he will run out of tiles."

A muffled voice replied to this last command but the Sergeant could not make out what was said so called out, "what was that? can you repeat that please?"

A voice came back saying, "nothing sarge, pulling back now."

Twenty-Two

"Right, where are we?" Said Garner, who was now sitting in the team's office with Parsons and Brierton having returned from the tea break in the station's canteen.

Parsons started by saying, "I have the results from Rachael Howton about the wine glasses found in the victim's living room. She says that she has tested for both the victim's and Anita Pemble's DNA and found both were present. But, the results from tests carried out on the victim showed that she had no alcohol present in her blood. Which suggests she had not drunk any wine the night before she was killed."

Garner said, "that's odd. Why would the glasses be there then?"

Brierton chipped in and said, "yes, it does seem odd at the very least. Especially as the house was very neat and tidy. You would think she would have washed them up either the night before or before she went out for her walk with the dog."

Garner then said, "have we got anything more on the possibility of a relationship between Anita Pemble and the victim? The victim's sister felt the idea was preposterous, so did anybody other than," Garner paused for a moment while he looked at the notes he had on his desk and then continued, "Sasha Bryon, that's the name of the lady that mentioned the affair, right."

Brierton said, "yes, that's her."

Parsons said, "that's what I wanted to bring up with you both. I went through all the notes from the house-to-house and it may mean nothing but the couple of people who also mentioned the affair all seemed to only know about it from things that Sasha had said to them. None of them seemed to know the details first hand."

"That's interesting," Brierton said and

Garner carried on by saying, "so, there is no evidence of anything going on between them, in fact, from what the sister said the complete opposite is more likely to be the truth."

Parsons replied, "looks that way."

The team were left with even more questions without answers now as everything they thought that was leading them to a quick conclusion for this case was becoming more confusing. They spent the next couple of hours quietly looking through all their notes and the notes from the house-to-house enquiries that Parsons had collated and printed off copies for Garner and Brierton.

As they sat reading, the door to the office opened and in walked one of the officers who had been involved with the incident that had taken place earlier in the day between the runner and the dog walker.

"Sir," he said, "just to update you on that runner's alibi, earlier."

Garner looked up and said, "go on then, help us out and tell us they have confessed to the People's Park killing."

The officer's face dropped and he said, "sorry, cannot help on that one. It turned out that the runner was just running home from work after a night shift at the hospital, so they had come from the completely wrong direction for your case."

Garner said, "oh well, there was always a chance, thanks for letting us know."

The officer replied to this with, "no problem sir, we always try to help if we can," and then turned around and headed back out of the office.

Brierton then said, "so, everything seems to take us nowhere really. The glasses being in the living room makes no sense, there is a big question mark about anything going on between Anita and the victim and another question mark about Anita and Edward's dog lead being in their house."

Brierton looked around the room at both Garner and Parsons who both looked as puzzled as she was.

Twenty-Three

So they could take a breather from the case and a change of surroundings for a while, the team had now made their way to the station canteen for a tea break.

As they drank their drinks, Brierton said.

"I have just had a thought, when we interviewed Edward, he said he had passed the dog stuff onto someone else to get rid of the items for them. We never asked him who that was. I am now wondering if there may be some relevance to who that was and the lead being found in his bedroom."

Garner said, "that's a good point, call down to the reception desk as he will probably still be sitting in the interview room and ask someone to pop along and ask him."

Brierton nods and starts to call the station's reception desk.

"Hello, this is DS Brierton."

While Brierton made her call, Garner and Parsons carried on talking about the case.

Brierton had now ended her call and said, "they are going to go and ask him and then call me back."

Garner, Brierton and Parsons started to make their way back to their office but got stopped at the canteen door by a group of people coming in dressed in running outfits.

Brierton turned to Parsons and said, "have you got a copy of the image of that runner captured on camera running near the park?"

Parsons said, "yes, I have it on my phone. Hang on, I'll get it," he then got his phone and opened the image on the screen and turned his phone towards Brierton to let her view the image.

Brierton studied the image, thought for a

moment, and then said, "I knew I had seen that outfit somewhere before. It's what one of the decorators was wearing at Sasha Bryon's house, the lad who she seemed to be flirting with was wearing it."

Just as she was talking, Brierton's phone started to ring so she answered it and said, "DS Brierton."

Brierton listened to the caller for a few seconds and then ended the call.

"Sir," Brierton had finished her call and was once again talking to Garner, "one of the reception staff went along and asked Edward who they had given the dog lead to," she paused and then said, "it was Sasha, they gave the stuff to Sasha Bryon."

Twenty-Four

When Garner and Brierton arrive at Sasha Bryon's house there was a uniformed officer already standing at the door.

Garner said to the officer, "is Sasha Bryon here?"

The officer replied, "yes, sir. It looks like she was packing to leave when we arrived. Her mother was taken to hospital last night and died during the night. I hear that the other half of the duo Peter has been located at his house as well and been arrested because he tried to do a runner."

Garner said, "thanks, can you tell the others to hold Peter at his place until we are finished here."

The officer at the door replied, "OK, I'll let them know."

As this short conversation came to an end, Garner and Brierton both entered the house and made their way to the kitchen at the rear of the property where they could hear people talking.

As they entered the kitchen Sasha shouted, "what is going on here, why am I being stopped from leaving?"

Brierton said, "morning, we will explain all this to you but first of all I would like to say how sorry we are to hear about the death of your mother."

Sasha looked around the room and then said, "thanks, she has been ill for a while so it was not a surprise but, I don't see why that has to stop me from going away."

Garner said, "it doesn't, but we want to talk to you about the death of Miriam in the park."

Sasha said, "I already told you I know nothing about that so I still do not understand what is going on here."

Garner replied to this, "well, we think you and Peter know a lot more about the death than your letting on so we would like you to come with us to the station to answer some more questions."

Sasha seemed to get very angry at this point and shouted, "well, that's not going to happen is it."

Garner said, "well it is," and turning to Brierton he said, "looks like we are going to have to arrest her to make sure she comes with us so, she's all yours." And started to walk out of the kitchen, leaving Brierton and the officers present to make the arrest and then transport Sasha back to the station.

As Garner got back to the front door of the house he paused where the officer was standing at the door and said, "can you get the others to bring Peter into the station now and get them to wait in the car park until they see us arrive with Sasha."

As Garner spoke, Brierton and another officer leading Sasha by the arm passed and Sasha was taken to a waiting police van that was now parked on the driveway of the house. Once Sasha had been safely placed in the van, Brierton returned to where Garner was standing and handed him some paperwork and plane tickets which he looked at and said.

"what's this?"

Brierton replied, "it's a copy of Sasha's mother Geraldine's will. It was in the bag Sasha was packing. I think it shows there is a great motive for the killing of Miriam."

As they walked down the driveway of the house, Garner read through the paperwork and as they got to the end of the drive he said, "your right, this gives us a possible motive. Can you get onto the officers at Peter's house and see if there are some tickets there as well? They might have been planning to travel together or meet up somewhere else."

Twenty-Five

The car park of the Grimsby police station was usually a busy place with vehicles coming and going. Today was no exception. Two marked vans were sitting side by side waiting for the arrival of Garner and Brierton. In one of the vans was Peter and the in the other was Sasha.

Garner had asked for them both to be held in the van until his arrival back at the station.

As Garner drove into the car park he pulled up and said to Brierton, "you get out here and hang around near the vans and I will park up. Hopefully, them seeing that we have both of them will help get one of them talking when we interview them."

Brierton got out of the car and made her

way towards the vans. And once Garner had parked his car, he made his way to the back entrance of the station to wait for Sasha and Peter to be brought in.

Peter was helped out of the van he had been brought to the station in and the officers with him started to take him towards the station. As this was done, Sasha was also escorted out of the van she had arrived in and taken towards the station a few meters behind Peter.

Hearing doors closing behind him, Peter turned and saw Sasha walking with two officers behind him. He tried to pull away from the officers with him in an attempt to get closer to Sasha but the officers had a good grip on his arms and were able to prevent him from getting away from them. Realising he could not get away from his escorts, Peter called out.

"Sasha, we will sort all of this out and then we can go away together."

The officer leading Peter into the station said, "be quiet."

Garner watched Sasha while Peter was calling out to her and noticed she said something in response to Peter but not loud enough to be heard by either Garner or Peter.

Once Peter and Sasha had both been taken into the station Brierton who had been standing near the van Sasha had been brought to the station in and had now made her way to where Garner was standing said, "Well, that was interesting."

Garner said, "yes, I wanted to see their reaction if they saw each other being brought into the station. That's why I asked for them both to be held out here until we arrived. Did you hear what Sasha said when Peter was calling out to her?"

"Yes," said Brierton, "she said, in your dreams mate. So it looks like she has been leading him on about getting together in the future."

Garner said, "which will hopefully help to get him talking. All we have to do is convince him that there was never any real chance for him with her and I think he will tell us everything we need to know."

Twenty-Six

Sasha and Peter were sitting in interview rooms opposite each other in the corridor with their legal representatives. Garner and Brierton were in the team's office getting ready and deciding how they were going to carry out the interviews. Once they were ready, they headed down and entered the interview room where Sasha was sitting.

They both sat down at the table and Brierton started the recording machine and announced who was in the room.

Garner then started the interview with, "right then, I don't think this will take us long. Can you explain your involvement with the death of Miriam?"

Sasha replied, "no comment."

Garner then said, "we expected this would be a no-comment interview so we will tell you what we think and how we have come to those conclusions and then you can either say something or not."

Brierton then started to speak. "We have found the copy of your mum's will in the bag you had packed along with the two New York flight tickets."

Sasha just sat in silence and stony-faced. So Brierton continued.

"We think you and Peter arranged to kill Miriam Parris between you. Although, we expect Peter is not aware of your real plans. So, we expect him to be more forthcoming with the events that took place in the park and your involvement with them."

Again, Sasha just sat in silence and shrugged her shoulders.

Garner decided at this point that there was no point carrying on with this interview as it was obvious Sasha was not going to tell them anything. So he turned to Brierton and said, "I think it's time to go and speak to Peter about this now.

Please wait here as we will be back soon and probably in a position to charge you with your part in all of this."

Once Garner had finished speaking, Brierton said, "OK, sir. I am terminating this interview, " and turned off the recording system.

Twenty-Seven

As Garner and Brierton walked across the corridor Peter's legal adviser was approaching the interview room where Peter was sitting and waiting to be interviewed.

"Have you just got here?" asked Brierton. To which the legal adviser answered, "no, just a call of nature."

Brierton said, "oh, OK, well come in and get started then."

All three entered the room, Garner and Brierton sat down at the table on the opposite side to where Peter had now been joined by his legal help.

Brierton switched on the recording device and said, "interview with Peter Clarke concerning the death of Miriam Parris also present is Peter Clarke's legal representative, DCI Garner and DS Brierton."

Once the interview recording was started Garner said, "Peter, we want to speak to you about the death of Miriam Parris in the People's Park yesterday in the early hours of the morning. Do you have anything you want to tell us about that?"

Peter looked at Garner and then his legal adviser and said, "no comment."

"Right, OK, we expected that as it is the same response we got from Sasha when we spoke to her about this matter. So as with her we will tell you what we think has been going on and then you can decide if you want to talk to us or not."

Garner then paused to give Peter time to think about what he had just said and then nodded to Brierton to indicate that she should take over at this point.

Brierton started by opening her folder and taking out the copy of Geraldine's will and placing it in front of Peter. She then said, "This is a copy of Geraldine's will which shows that on her death her estate would have to be divided equally between Sasha and another person. Did you know about this?"

Peters' legal adviser said, "I am not sure what this has to do with my client. Even if he did know about the contents of the will, how does this relate to why he has been arrested and brought here today."

Brierton continued, "I am coming to that. You see, the other person is Miriam Parris. So again, I ask, did you know about this?"

Peter looked at his adviser again, who shook his head and when Peter looked back at Brierton he said, "no comment."

Garner said, "fine, " and looking at Brierton said, "just go through what we have and Peter can just interrupt if he feels inclined to do so."

Brierton said, "OK. We are waiting for test results on fibres found at the scene to see if they match a similar tracksuit we found at your house and as we speak officers are visiting Miriam, Anita and Edward's houses to see if the keys we found in your house allow them entry into their houses as we know you had worked in their houses recently."

Garner interrupted Brierton and asked Peter if he had anything to add but Peter just shook his head so Brierton carried on.

"We also have these." Brierton took the travel tickets out of the folder and placed them down on the table in front of Peter. "These tickets are for flights to New York."

Peter looked at the tickets and realising it was not his name on them became very agitated and said, "I don't understand. She was supposed to be going to New York with me but these tickets are for her and Sam, my boss."

Brierton interjected by saying, "well, it looks like you are not as important to her as you thought you were."

Peter became even more agitated when Garner said this to him. "No, that's not true, she is in love with me and said, we would go away and start a new life away from here when she inherited everything from her mum."

Brierton said, "so was the plan to get rid of Miriam so Sasha would inherit everything? Because looking at those tickets she was not planning a future with you, was she?"

Peter looked at his legal adviser and said, "can we speak?"

Brierton placed her finger on the stop button of the recording system and said, "interview suspended, "pressed the button and gathered up the items she had on the table and placed them back into her folder. Both Garner and Brierton then left the room to allow Peter to take some legal advice. As they left the room Garner said, "give us a shout when you ready to talk."

Twenty-Eight

Brierton and Parsons were sitting in the team's office waiting for Garner to join them. They had been given a written statement made by Peter that was a full confession about the killing of Miriam Parris. It stated that Sasha was upset about her mother leaving half of her estate to Miriam in the event of her death. He claimed that Sasha had promised they would run away together because she was in love with him and wanted to start a new life with him in America.

The statement continued by giving details of how Sasha had kept the wine glasses from a previous evening at Miriam's house and how she had got Peter to plant them in Miriam's house. Sasha had kept the dog lead from when Anita and Edward Pemble's dog had died and they had asked Sasha to get rid of the dog things for them. Peter had also planted this in the Pemble's house after he had used it to kill Miriam.

Garner came into the office in what seemed to be a hurry. He sat down at his desk and Brierton told him about the confession Peter had made.

Garner said, "that's brilliant. Has there been any mention of the other guy? You know Sam, the guy Sasha was planning to run off with."

Parsons said, "no, there does not seem to be any link between him and what the other two were up to. So it looks like he is completely innocent of anything other than planning to leave his wife and run off with Sasha. The interviewing officer said that when he was spoken to he seemed to have had no idea what had been going on at all."

Garner stood back up and said, "right Becca, can you get onto the Crown Prosecution Service and give them all the information we have, and see what they say? I don't think it's worth taking bets on this as I think there will be two murder charges coming up. One for Peter Clarke and the other for Sasha Bryon."

Brierton replied, "I will get onto it straight away."

As Brierton finished speaking, Garner's mobile rang so he took it out of his pocket and answered the call.

"Hello ma'am, how can I help?" He said, and after a short time spent listening, he ended the call.

Garner started to leave the room and as he did he said, "give me a call as soon as you hear back from them. I have had a message to go and see Superintendent Jones so we can discuss what is going on with the court case in London.

Twenty-Nine

Superintendent Jones and Elena Bendel were sitting in the Superintendent's office talking while they waited for Garner to join them. Elena had flown up from London earlier in the day specially to debrief Garner on events in London.

Garner entered the office and said, "sorry to keep you both waiting, we have just wrapped up the People's Park murder case."

Jones said, "that's fine Robert, well done for solving that one, and, please pass on my thanks to the rest of the team."

Elena then said, "please join us DCI Garner, and I will give you the details of what has been going on in London."

Garner sat down beside Elena and she

started to explain what had taken place during the court case that Garner had been waiting to take place for a long time now.

Elena said, "well, you will be glad to know that everything went according to plan, to be honest, things worked out better than expected."

Garner said, "sounds good."

Elena continued, "the information you got during the interview you carried out with Kurzwell led to some more arrests as I think you know, but information gleaned from those arrests led to further arrests. In total, there were nine senior figures from the London crime scene taken into custody, with seven of them being charged with offences carried out during the reign of the original crime family you dealt with and all of them being charged with offences carried out more recently."

Jones said, "so, are you saying you have cleared up open cases that a more recent?"

Elena replied, "yes, quite a few."

As Elena was going to carry on speaking, there was a knock on the office door.

Jones called out, "come in." She paused as the door opened and her assistant entered the office carrying a tray with a large coffee pot and cups on it. Jones continued to speak, "I thought we may need some refreshments."

Elena said, "that's very kind of you."

Once the assistant had placed the tray down on a lower table at the end of the Superintendent's desk and left, Elena started to speak again.

"As I was saying, we have cleared up about thirty open cases which we knew were linked to the people arrested, we had never been able to prove anything. However, once they realised that all of them had been arrested it was just a matter of time before one or two of them broke ranks and looked for a way out of spending most of the rest of their lives in prison."

Garner then said, "that's all brilliant, so how many years did they get between them?"

To which Elena replied, "just under one hundred and seventy years between them. There have been intimations made to their solicitors that there could be some reductions off their sentences if they help clear up further cases but we are not holding out much hope on that."

Jones said, "so what about Kurzwell then? He has been a thorn in our side for a good few years."

Elena said, "he is now serving his time in solitary, he is only going to be inside for a couple of years. I know you would have liked him to get a lot more and to be honest so would I but without his help we would not have been able to clear up so many cases."

Garner said, "well at least he will be out of our hair now."

Elena replied, "true, you should never see or hear from him again as once he has served his time he will be going into witness protection and will eventually be living overseas somewhere."

Jones then got up from her desk and said, "I think we should leave the coffee here and head down to the pub for a celebration. Robert, go and get your team and join us as they played a part in all of this as well."

Garner stood up and said, "will do ma'am, see you at the bar."

Kurzwell

Mick Kurzwell was preparing to spend the next few years of his life in solitary confinement. This was the safest way for him to serve out his time in prison before entering the witness protection system and vanishing for the rest of his life under a new identity. This of course was quite a change in his life that had started many years before on the streets where he grew up and learnt how to look after himself as the child of parents who were drunks and drug addicts.

Back then, school was a dirty word for people like him so his classroom was out and about and the lessons he had to attend were a lot harder than the ones in school. He would be used by teenagers to shoplift for them and once he was old enough to travel around the area unnoticed, he became a runner for the local drug dealers.

As time went on and Kurzwell got further and further into the gang life around him he realised that to survive, he would have to get as high up in the pecking order as he could and get as tough as possible so he could look after himself. So, he started to look at the people above him and work out how to either get around them or in some cases get rid of them. This was the attitude that got him noticed by the local dealers and eventually one of them took him under their wing so they could make the most of his talents.

They started by sending him to a house where some of his mates hung out and he had to talk them into getting their hits from his bosses rather than their current suppliers who ran the house they went to for their hits. This was quite easy because he had been told he could undercut the current supplier's prices. What he didn't realise was, that the times he got caught trying to poach users, it was him that had to take the beating. Because this started to happen more often than not, he took another decision that as soon as he was old enough to leave home without social services pestering him again, he would do so. This decision eventually led him to London and join one of the most powerful and dangerous crime families in the world as an enforcer.

This move had been a great one for him as he was now part of a more organised and controlled organisation. The potential to be killed or arrested and sent to prison was a lot higher than before but, however, he had people who he could now trust to have his back. All he had to do was keep his nose clean as far as his bosses were concerned and abide by the unwritten rules of the family. These were quite simple really.

'Do as your told and keep your mouth shut.'

Kurzwell found living by these simple rules easy, after all, it was the way he grew up.

Things only really started to change when he was ordered to do hits on people, that he thought were no real threat to the family and were just attempts to scare people who might try and take them down. For some reason, even with all the punishment beatings and killings he had carried out in the past, hurting people because they may be dangerous to the organisation in the future was not right in his books. He spoke to who he thought was someone he could trust about this, but all it got him was a beating from another enforcer and he was then living under the constant threat of being killed for doing something that was seen as being against the family. This is when he decided it was time to get out and try and start a new life.

The next couple of years were probably the hardest of his life, as he spent time gathering and recording evidence that he planned to use against the family he worked for. He knew that doing so could lead to him being killed but he had come to terms with either, getting out or being killed. Either way, he was out.

As time went on, Kurzwell realised the police were closing in on the heads of the family and it would be in his best interests to either run and hide, or give the police just enough to bring down the family but allow him to get away from London and maybe start again back home. Mind you, he didn't believe for one moment that this was possible as the slightest suspicion that he was behind the downfall of the family bosses, and he would've had a price on his head forever.

It was about this time that Kurzwell first encountered Bob Garner, who then was a member of the team tasked with breaking up the London crime family and putting as many of them as possible behind bars. Until now, Garner had never been in, on an interview with Kurzwell. This is because, it has now become apparent that Kurzwell had fed the team information that had led to most of the top family members being arrested and convicted. Garner now knew that it was probably the National Crime Agency that had taken the lead when it came to Kurzwell and that is why they had now come to another deal with him.

The real trouble had started for Kurzwell when some of the family members in London worked out it could only be him that had informed on them and that is why they had approached him to help get the new route for smuggling drugs into the country through Immingham and once that was up and running, they planned was to kill him.

About the Author

John Messingham was born in Hampton, Middlesex, England. After finishing school, he joined the British Army and served as an Infantryman and later trained as a radio operator within the battalion mortar platoon. After his time in the army, he trained as a computer programmer and started a long career in IT. The fiction he writes sometimes draws on both his military and IT backgrounds.

For more information about John and his writing, please visit

https://johnmessingham.co.uk

By John Messingham

DCI Garner and DS Brierton Novelettes

Series One

The Pier

The Body in the Van

Murder in the Park

Short Stories

The Water Thieves

Reece Leach Short Stories One

The Watchers

Printed in Great Britain
by Amazon